## HODDER CHILDREN'S BOOKS

First published in Great Britain in 2021 by Hodder & Stoughton

5 7 9 10 8 6 4

A CIP catalogue record for this book is available from the British Library.

ISBN 978 1 444 95169 1

Printed and bound in Great Britain by Clays Ltd, Elcograf S.p.A

The paper and board used in this book are made from wood from responsible sources.

MIX
Paper from
responsible sources
FSC® C104740

Hodder Children's Books
An imprint of
Hachette Children's Group
Part of Hodder & Stoughton Limited
Carmelite House
50 Victoria Embankment
London EC4Y 0DZ

An Hachette UK Company
www.hachette.co.uk
www.hachettechildrens.co.uk

# SCRIBBLE WITCH

## Paper friends

Spellings and doodlings
by Inky Willis

**h** HODDER

For...

# CHAPTER ONE

This is my class.

me ↑ Chloe-shaped hole

That's Mr Stilton, my teacher. You get used to him.

And that funny hole there is where my best friend used to be. Chloe left Dungfields to go to Lady Juniper's School for Girls. But it's OK. We still write notes to each other all the time, thanks to our *other* friend. **(Who, by the way, just happens to be a little paper witch.)**

*She's* a bit of a mystery. I kind of just found her. She was drawn on a bit of paper, stuck inside this tatty old dictionary. I cut her out and ... ta-da!

That's her!

Captain Purrkins

She's invisible (to other people) and just really, REALLY amazing. She flies our notes about, and she talks in notes too, and I bet you can't guess what she's called. **(Notes!)**

This is one of her notes that I keep in my pencil case because I like it so much.

I is soooo happYing when friendling Molly does curvy banana-shape happy lips!

(I mean, how cute is that?)

Chloe and I have to be careful, though. She's only tiny and very fragile so rule number one is this:

We NEVER ask Notes and Captain Purrkins to deliver notes if it's raining (not since we very almost had a HUMONGOUS tragedy). Water and paper do not mix. Or they mix too well. Either way we don't want our paper friend turning into mushy pulp.

Anyway, rain is a no-no. More than a no-no. It's a no-no-no-no-never-ever-no! So, when we had a few rainy days, I didn't write to Chloe at all.

This was the last note she sent before the rain came:

Molly!

No more notes!

Sky's getting dark.
                    Might rain.

I repeat:

# DANGER!
## NO MORE NOTES!

P.S. What are you having for lunch today?

Love Chloe x

And then it *did* rain. It rained then stopped

then rained then stopped for

# THREE WHOLE VERY ANNOYING DAYS!

So I couldn't write back, and that was extremely

rubbish.


On rainy day number two I was busy sighing

and grimacing when Notes wrote this:

Is you down in the dumpings because of no Chloe notes?

So then I felt bad. Because I *was* down in the dumpings. I mean dumps. Even though I absolutely *shouldn't* have been.

(I had a magic scribble witch in my pen pot and the cutest little mini cat to stroke. What more did I want?!)

I wrote back ...

I'm fine x

... but I'm pretty sure she knew I was lying.

suspicious face

And by rainy day three, I couldn't hide it any more.

I was sitting with my friend, Emily, in the book corner. And I could feel my face doing that dull-eyed thing cows do when they're chewing grass. And my body was all slouched over like a zombie (one with really heavy shoulders).

Emily was too busy reading to notice.

We were sharing a book called **Mysteries of Ancient Egypt** because ancient Egypt is our new class topic. We've got to do "independent research" for our "independent projects".

(I am OK with this, but Emily is in total project heaven.)

So we were both holding the book and Emily was going **oooh** and **whoa** and **wow** at literally every sentence.

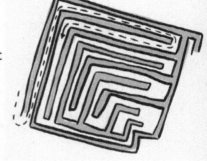

Not me, though. I didn't really care what had happened to that big

lost

maze or the

gold-faced king or that big no-nose lion thing.

What *I* cared about was what Chloe was up to.

Anyway, I must have looked really grim
because Notes flew over on
her magic pencil
to give me a
nose hug.

(That's what she
does when I'm sad.)

Afterwards she stayed close by, playing
dustball football with Captain Purrkins.

(Did I mention he's magically
invisible too? Oh, and he's also
sometimes a pencil topper.
It's complicated.)

"Molly, are you even listening?!" said Emily, who had possibly been talking at me for quite a long time.

"Uh. Sorry. Was thinking about ... er ..." I said.

"Well, pay attention," she sighed. "I'm trying to help you improve your project."

"Oh. Thanks. I think."

Emily gets irritated with me quite a lot. I like her and (I think) she likes me, but we're very, very, very, very, very, very (times by for ever) different. And we definitely annoy each other a bit.

I once asked Emily to tell me her top ten annoying things about me (because I really like top tens) and she said I was "*being utterly ridiculous again*".

So then I wrote it anyway and just pretended I was her.

# TOP TEN ANNOYING THINGS ABOUT MOLLY MILLS
### (written as if I'm Emily):

10. Molly is utterly ridiculous. ← Emily is the only person I know who says "utterly".

9. Molly often gets hard maths questions right by total accident. ← FALSE. I'm just quite good at maths and Emily hates it when I know stuff she doesn't. Even though it doesn't happen very often.

8. Molly's pencil case looks shifty.

My pencil case looks fabulous.

7. Molly is sometimes careless and makes silly mistakes just because she doesn't bother to concentrate.

This literally never happens.

oops!

5. Molly is very occasionally very slightly grouchy.

But only for very good reasons.

4. Molly keeps writing notes in class.

← Can't argue with that.

3. Molly sometimes forgets to learn her spellings.

←We have different priorities.

2. Molly is a trouble magnet.

To be fair this is mostly a problem for Molly (me)!

That's it. There is no number one.

Molly is really not very annoying at all.

Anyway, by this point Emily had worked out I wasn't reading or listening.

"If you're not interested, I'll have this," she said, and she took the book for herself. Bit rude.

But I couldn't be bothered to argue so instead I did the zombie-cow thing again, and I stared at my knees.

They weren't very interesting. Not until Notes started writing on them with her magic pencil.

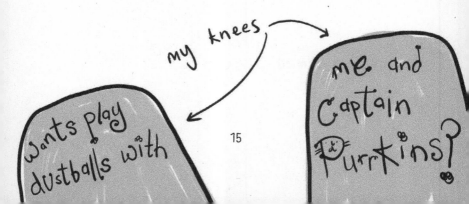

I shook my head. I was too mopey to play.

Rain was still pinging off the windows and I was *so* certain this would be another rubbish day.

But get this ... I was *so* wrong!

Because, just then, there was a neat

# rat-a-tat

knock on the classroom door.

"Come in!" sighed Mr Stilton.

The door opened.

Mrs Oddments, the school secretary, was
standing there. And she wasn't alone.

"Mr Stilton," she said, "you have a neeyoopeeyoopul!" (That's how Mrs Oddments says "new pupil".)

A girl stepped forward and offered to shake Mr Stilton's hand. It was a grown-up kind of move, and she reminded me of someone, but I couldn't think who.

"Hello," she said. "I'm Amelie. And I'm utterly delighted to meet you."

Utterly?! Who did I know that said "utterly" …?

Ah, who cared! Either way,

# neeyoopeeyoopuls

are the best!

And, thanks to Amelie, zombie-cow Molly was turning back into excited normal human Molly.

from this → to this →

# CHAPTER TWO

Mrs Oddments left and Notes started scribbling

on the floor:

New bestest friendling for Molly?

I smiled but shook my head.

See, I used to be a bit obsessed with getting a

new best friend to replace Chloe. But I'm over it. Chloe doesn't need replacing. She's still my best friend even if she's at a different school. And I've got other non-best (but still very nice) friends here at Dungfields.

The class was super silent as we listened to Amelie and Mr Stilton.

"Shall I introduce myself to the class?" said Amelie.

"Why not?" said Mr Stilton in a bored "seen it all before" kind of voice.

"Back in your seats, snotbags!" he shouted
(or something similar).

"Sit down and pipe down."

Amelie didn't seem at all bothered that her new teacher was rude and beardy. And she wasn't bothered about standing up at the front of the class either, even though she didn't know anyone. She just waited for us to get to our tables, then propped her hands on her hips and began.

"I'll just say a little about me," she said, all loud and smiley and crazy brave! (I'd never be able to stand in front of loads of strangers and chat like that.)

"I'm a judo brown belt and the Bogdale Junior Chess Champion. I love history and science, and one day I'll be an archaeologist."

Mr Stilton got her to explain what an archaeologist is (someone who digs up old stuff). And while Amelie chatted, Emily scribbled something on a bit of paper.

Bit of a show-off, isn't she?!

But Amelie wasn't really showing off. Not exactly. She was just being very — well — very ...

And then I got it. Amelie was being *Emily.*

Once I'd thought it, it was obvious! The confidence, the way she was best at loads of stuff ... the way she said "utterly" ...

Amelie was utterly Emily-ish. Not in a seeing-double kind of way. There were differences. For one thing Emily didn't have Amelie's happy smiley confidence. So it's not like they were identy-twins, just very, *very* similar.

As far as I knew, Emily had never, ever had a

best friend. Maybe this was her chance.

She's just ~~confidant~~ confident.
I think you'll like her when you
get to know her.

Doubt it.
We've nothing in
common.

Clearly Emily couldn't see it!

Everyone else could, though. All the kids *and* Mr Stilton too. They were looking from Amelie to Emily and back again, mouths open, eyebrows high with amazement.

Notes was stunned too. She pulled a scrap of paper from my notebook.

Same same ?!
Amelie is Emily?!!

I wrote on the back:

No, but I know EXACTLY what you mean.

Eventually Amelie stopped talking.

Marvin clapped and shouted, "You're an archaeologist and I dig it!"

Mr Stilton ignored Marvin. He looked about the class and scratched his beard. "Where to put you ...?" he said.

I couldn't help it. My hand shot up in the air and I called out, "Over here! Next to Emily!"

And everyone murmured and nodded. Because it was SO OBVIOUS! Emily and Amelie were made for each other.

Anyway, Notes thought it was a good idea.

Good thinkings !

So at least someone appreciated my match-making efforts.

"Well, it's a bit of a squeeze," said Mr Stilton. "But, fine. You and Marvin shuffle round. Make room. We'll sort you out with a locker later."

He moved a chair over so Amelie could sit down next to Emily. (Emily shuffled her pencil case over politely, but I could tell she wasn't happy.)

tense jaw

Super straight back →

steam coming out of nostrils

(not really)

Amelie pulled a big heavy bag from her shoulders, pulled out a crazy-cool pencil case and placed it neatly on the table.

(like Emily's but shinier)

"As you're a history fan, you'll like our new topic," said Mr Stilton. "We're learning about ancient Egypt."

"Oh, I know," she said. "The secretary mentioned it to my mum yesterday, so I've made a few notes."

Amelie pulled a huge ring binder from her bag and dropped it on the table with a

BOOM!

The class gasped as one.

Emily's eyes nearly popped out of her head. She looked at me again and mouthed the words "show-off!", which I ignored.

Emily's not normally mean. It was weird!

"That's *a few notes*?" said Mr Stilton.

"Oh ... should I have done more?" Amelie asked. She looked genuinely worried.

"No, that's, er, fine," replied Mr Stilton. The red pen he used for marking twitched in his fingers. He looked a little bit pale and frazzled for a second. But then he snapped out of it and said (in his most un-fun voice) that we could have a **"QUICK FUN QUIZ"** before break time.

"We've got ten minutes. Let's see if any of you

grimy grotters have learnt anything!"

(Well, that's more or less what he said.)

I smiled at Amelie to reassure her, but she was too busy arranging her stationery to notice.

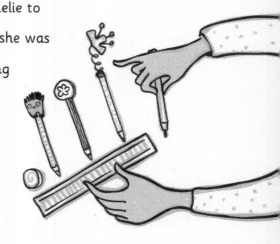

(She even measured the distance between her pencils with a ruler.
**So Emily!**)

And then Emily saw me smiling at Amelie and her eyes narrowed like this.

smile —

not appreciated

Anyway, we had to work as a table team, and we had to choose a name.

*Great*, I thought. *A chance to get to know Amelie!*

Emily was bound to like her once they got chatting.

Marvin said, "Hi, new friend!" to Amelie.

And I said, "Hi," too, and I told her our names.

So then Emily had to say something so she didn't look super rude.

"Would you like to choose our team name?" she asked Amelie (which I thought was a good and **friendly** sign).

Amelie said, "No, you go ahead." (Another good sign.)

And then Emily said, "Cleopatra?"

But Amelie said, "Or maybe something a bit less obvious?" And she didn't say it in a horrible way, but it made Emily's jaw tighten.

"The Great Sphinx then," said Emily.

"Oh! What about 'Bastet'?! She's the cat goddess," said Amelie.

35

Emily gritted her teeth and said, "I know who she is."

And then Notes started scribbling like mad on the table.

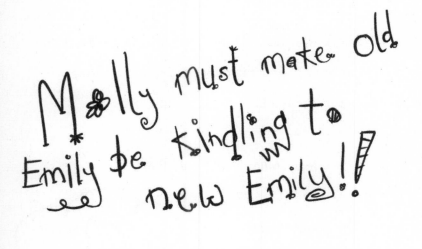

I couldn't write back without being seen so I just shrugged and looked a bit useless.

Then, when Mr Stilton called over to ask what our team name was, Amelie and Emily went totally quiet.

"Well?" he said.

Someone had to say something. *I* had to say something.

# "THE GREAT STINKS!"

I said. "I mean spinks! No, not spinks ... finks?!"

But it was too late. We were The Great Stinks. And, if it's possible, Emily looked even madder than she did before.

# CHAPTER THREE

The Great Stinks won the quiz by the way.

To be fair we couldn't *lose*. The only two people who knew anything about anything were on our team.

Emily somehow knew when the earliest ancient Egyptians were *living*. And Amelie named about a trillion gods and goddesses.

Actually, Amelie put her hand up for everything, even stuff *Emily* didn't know. It was crazy impressive.

Notes thought so too.

New Emily has such wondrous cleverings!

Yeah.
Amelie is supersmart.

But why is old Emily has scowley cross face at new Emily?

She really wasn't
getting the
whole *totally
different
people* thing.

No idea why Emily's being grumpy. So strange. Hope Amelie doesn't notice.

Luckily Amelie was too busy answering quiz questions to notice. But Notes was right. Emily was not *at all* happy.

And neither was Mr Stilton.

# *"This is pure laziness!"*

he said. "I can count on two fingers the number of children who've done any independent learning!" And it was obvious who he meant. Me and Marvin. (Just kidding. He meant Amelie and Emily.)

"We're visiting the ancient Egypt exhibition tomorrow," he said. "So, here's some playtime homework. I want each of you to think of a question you'd like to answer at the museum. We'll make a class list. Now get out of my sight!"

Urgh. Playtime homework! (It didn't even make sense. Isn't homework meant to happen at home?)

I'm pretty sure it's illegal to make kids think about work stuff during playtimes. Who did Mr Stilton think he was? The Dungfields pharaoh?!

Anyway, that wasn't the worst thing about

going out in the rain. The worst thing was having to leave Notes in class.

"Back soon," I whispered, tugging my raincoat from my locker.

Notes scribbled (invisibly) across my locker door:

And I wanted to ask her not to (because when Notes helps it's not always very helpful), but the whole locker area was getting really crowded. Plus, Notes had already flown off to the book corner to get started.

So I just crossed my fingers and went out into the drizzle.

Normally everyone splits into little groups and pairs at playtime, but this playtime we were just one big clump of kids. Everyone (not Emily) crowded around Amelie wanting to know stuff.

WHERE ARE YOU FROM?

"Snoddlington."

(That's a village next to Bogdale.)

Got any brothers or sisters?

"One grown-up sister. No brothers."

What team do you support?

"Huh?"

Are you, like, a **GENIUS** or something?

"It's possible but unlikely."

(She totally is!)

Can you teach us your judo moves?

"Not really."

CAN YOU SHOW US YOUR CHESS MOVES?

"Er ... how?"

Can you show us your arky ... arky ...

"Archaeologist moves?"

Yeah, those!

Amelie paused. It was a silly question, so I figured she'd just say "no".

But then she said, "You mean you want me to dig stuff up?"

And because everyone (not Emily) was so hyper-excited, we all shouted, "Yes!"

I think Amelie must have felt sorry for us and our puny non-genius brains. Because she shrugged then looked about on the grass for a big fat stick.

"OK then," she said. "Anyone who wants to see some digging, follow me!"

She held the stick high and marched across the wet field with us (not Emily) cheering and

marching behind
her. We were like an
army, following our
leader into battle.

"Here!" she said, and she stopped by a conker
tree. "This is a good spot."

Then she started digging.

We circled around her and I held my breath.
Rain trickled down my neck and I didn't even
care. Because even though I knew we were
in Dungfields School, in Bogdale, part of me
thought maybe Amelie would find something
amazing in that sloppy mud. Something gold and
precious and anciently ancient.

A few minutes later, my fantasy had mostly

died a death. There was no treasure. Just a muddy hole, muddy Amelie and an oddly unhappy faraway (but not muddy) Emily.

"Sorry, guys. You didn't really expect me to find anything, did you?" said Amelie, seeing our disappointment. (Phew! It wasn't just me thinking Amelie was going to make us rich.)

And we all laughed, like "Nah, course not, that'd be crazy ..."

Then, because there was nothing better to do (and because some of us still kind of hoped we might find treasure), we all found sticks too. And we dug our own muddy holes.

That's a whole class of kids (not Emily) digging holes. Twenty-nine holes! If there was treasure to be found, we'd find it!

But nope. This is what we found:

23 rocks (not shown)

1 tiny bone

1 glue stick lid

1 plastic straw

...and lots of mud (also not shown)

Then, when most of us had given up, Mia yelled, "There's something here!" And we all rushed over.

It was hard to see properly because everyone was pushing, but I could hear Mia's stick tapping on something in the mud.

"Let Amelie see!" said Marvin. "She's the

## ARCHAEOPTERYX!"

"She's a flying dinosaur?" said Alfie.

(I think Marvin meant archaeologist.)

Anyway, everyone moved aside to let Amelie inspect the whatever-it-was.

She gently pushed the dirt off, then she rubbed it with the corner of her jumper.

"It's metal!" she said.

We all gasped. Metal could only mean one thing ...

# ANCIENT EGYPTIAN GOLD!!!!

Spoiler alert: it wasn't ancient Egyptian gold.

"It's kind of a dull grey," she said. "We just need to give it a bit of a wiggle then ..."

But there was no wiggling, because while we'd been busy staring at the ground, Mr Grimmers (our grizzly caretaker) had come over.

**"What in Bogdale's name d'ya think you're playing at?!?!?!?"** he said.

Mr Grimmers is boomy and huge and hairy and very slightly terrifying.

I could feel the blood rushing out of my face. (Though I was probably too muddy for anyone to notice.)

For a mini moment we all just froze.

Then someone spoke.

Amelie.

"This is my fault, sir," she said. "I'm sorry. Would you like me to take a detention?"

# WHOA! NO ONE had ever, EVER asked for a detention before.

Amelie took brave to a whole new level!

Mr Grimmers' nostrils flared.

"And who," he said, "are you?!"

If Amelie was nervous, she hid it really, *really* well.

"I'm Amelie," she said. "I'm new."

He shook his head and muttered something to himself.

Then he said, "Just gerroff my field, the lot of you. And don't let me catch you digging it up again! **Goddit?!**"

And with twenty-nine murmurs of, "Yes, Mr Grimmers," we trudged away from our treasure.

# CHAPTER FOUR

Emily joined us walking back to class.

I tried to tell her what had happened so she'd see she had the wrong idea about Amelie. It was a bit hard to explain, though, because everyone was talking really loudly. Saying words like "hero" and "legend".

Words that, possibly, Emily *really* didn't want to hear. (She literally didn't say anything the whole way back to our table.)

But Amelie *was* a hero *and* a legend. She'd

stood up for us all, even though the digging *wasn't* her idea. Even though it was her first day at Dungfields.

Though even hero Amelie couldn't save us from Mr Stilton.

"So, you mucky ratters!" he said (probably).

"What do we want to find out?"

Yikes! We'd all forgotten (or possibly ignored)
the probably illegal playtime homework!

All except for Notes. Unlike the rest of us,
she'd been hard at work.

Across the desks, over the walls, scrawled
across the ceiling, were questions!

It was written in invisible (not to me) magic pencil. And, OK, maybe not all the questions were that helpful, but they weren't unhelpful, so that was a HUGE relief.

Mr Stilton stood at the front of class, tapping the whiteboard with his pen.

**"Well?!"** he said.

Emily and Amelie both put their hands up (not a surprise). But Mr Stilton waved them down. "Someone else," he said.

A few kids slowly poked their fingers into the air, but none of them looked like they really meant it.

But then Marvin put his hands up (yes, both of them) and he did it with a huge enthusiastic grin. Marvin sometimes finds taking part in class stuff tricky. So when Marvin *does* take part, Mr Stilton has to pick him.

"Yes, Marvin?" said Mr Stilton.

"Something's hidden in the ground!"

Murmurs rippled around the room. Marvin wasn't talking about ancient Egypt. He was talking about the metal thing buried in the field. (But Mr Stilton didn't know that.)

"OK, good," said Mr Stilton. "Who can turn

that into a question? Something we can ask at
the museum? Molly?"

For the record I didn't have my hand up. I
was just unlucky enough to catch his eye.
(Which, by the way, is a really gross saying.)

eye catching
(didn't happen)

Anyway, I did my best ...

"We could ask *what* might be
hidden in the ground?" I said. "The
ground in Egypt, I mean."

But I wasn't really thinking all that much
about Egypt. I was thinking about the field and
the metal thing, wondering what *that* might be.

Anyway, between us, we managed to make a
short but not awful list. And Mr Stilton stopped
moaning.

Notes did a load of (invisible, of course) doodles

to go with the questions. She was really getting

into this Egyptian topic.

Afterwards, she flew back to her pen pot (where she lives) and I secretly snuck her some pencil shavings (her favourite food).

When no one was looking, she threw out a scrunched-up note.

Thankings! Pencil sharpenings is wondrous tasty!

I wrote on the back and dropped it into the pen pot.

You're welcome. Do you want to come to the museum ~~tommorow~~ tomorrow?

A new note followed.

Oh, yessings! Yes!!!
Notes loves secret mysteries
of Egypters. Notes' whole
life is a mystering!

Odd. I wasn't sure what she meant by that.
But I couldn't write back because Emily was
kicking me (not hard) under the table.

I mouthed, "What?"

And she slipped me a note.

What are your lunch arrangements? Will you be eating with me, as you have done for the past month? Or will you be eating with everyone's new best friend?

Huh? Can't we all eat together? What's your problem with Amelie?

I passed the note back and waited. There — I'd
said it. Straight to the point.

She answered superfast.

Fine.

Now I know
whose side
you're on.

But it wasn't really an answer at all. Just
more craziness!

I mean, *what* sides? Amelie hadn't done
anything wrong. *And* she was new. Poor Amelie!

This was getting weirder and weirder.

Don't be silly.
Just join us at the
picnic tables.

I pushed the note towards Emily, but she didn't even read it. She just scrunched it up and stuffed it into her pencil case. There were tears in her eyes.

What was going on???!!!!

"Emily!" I whispered.

But then Amelie and Marvin noticed she was upset too.

"What's the matter?" whispered Amelie.

(Emily ignored this.)

Then Marvin shouted,

**"EMILY'S CRYING!"** Really loud.

So suddenly everyone looked over.

"Emily?" said Mr Stilton. "Is something wrong?"

She sniffed then sat up straight. "I'm fine," she croaked. "I'd like to move seats, please."

Notes popped her
head out of the pen pot
and blinked at me, confused. But I didn't have
any idea what was going on either.

Notes scribbled on the table.

Old Emily is
Sads with mysterings!

I nodded. Something mysterious *was* making
Emily sad. (I think that's what Notes meant ...
sometimes it's hard to tell.)

Then, just like that, Emily stuffed her pencils

and pens in her pencil case, and she went to sit on Mustafa's table on the other side of the room.

Notes was watching the whole time. Her tiny eyebrows were tight with worry. But then her expression changed into a look of doodly determination.

She grabbed her magic pencil and flew to Mr Stilton's whiteboard. And above the class list she wrote this:

Most Urgentest mysterings of all: why is old Emily crossly-sads?

And she stood on top of the board, nodding,
hands on her scribbly hips.

Then, she poked a finger in the air like she'd
had an idea. And back to the board she flew.
Down to the bottom of the list this time.

This is what she wrote:

(And extra wonderings... who did draw Notes?
Notes is wishing she knowed!)

*That's* what she meant about her whole life
being a mystery. She wanted to know where
she came from!

So many puzzles. My head was a total

muddle. Muddy treasure, miserable Emily and the impossible mystery of my scribble witch friend.

Solving all these mysteries was going to take more than a museum trip. It was going to take a miracle.

# CHAPTER FIVE

By lunchtime the rain had cleared.
For the first time in aaaaaaaages the
sky was free, blue and even a bit rainbowy!

Notes and Captain Purrkins wanted to come
outside too. So they climbed into my pencil case
and came along for the ride.

I noticed some coloured cones dotted along
the edge of the field, which meant it was off
limits. And I guessed this had something to do
with our digging earlier.

What a pain. I really, really, really wanted to know what that metal thing was. But at least no one else could get to it either.

Anyway. Lunch.

Amelie had loads of kids wanting to sit with her, so I went looking for Emily.

But Marvin said Emily had taken her lunch to the Quiet Room. The Quiet Room is where you can go if you need some time out.
(To be honest I forget it's even there half the time.)

So, no Emily.

I ended up eating my lunch on a damp bench with Marvin **(great)** and a load of crumb-flicking Year Ones **(less great)**. Then, Marvin got a bit panicky when crumbs landed in his pasta. So *he* went to the Quiet Room too. Leaving me with the small people.

It was not my favourite lunch experience ever.

I ate with my right hand and batted away crumby missiles with my left. I'm sure I looked utterly (gah! Now *I'm* saying it) nuts.

A few bites and slurps later, I was ready to escape the food-flingers. I snatched up my

lunchbox and pencil case and went to the girls'
loos.

OK, just to be clear, this is not where I'd
normally choose to hang out, but I was on a
mission. I wanted to write to Chloe.

It had been soooooo looooooong. But I
couldn't write where I normally would. Normally
I'd hide in the Secret Spot
(a big hollow bush at the
far end of the field).
But, of course, I couldn't
get to the Secret Spot
because the field was out
of bounds. So the loos were
pretty much my only option.

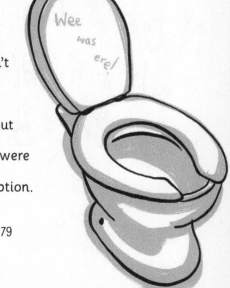

I found an empty cubicle and sat down on the toilet (lid down of course — yuck!). I unzipped my pencil case and Notes hopped out, followed by a sleepy Captain Purrkins.

Notes immediately covered her eyes. She fumbled around for her pencil then wrote across the cubicle wall.

Notes is not lookings! Notes is doing polite waitings while friendling Molly is on stink-bucket.

"It's fine," I whispered. "I'm not using the toilet. I just need somewhere I can write to Chloe without people asking questions."

She slowly risked opening one eye, then the other. Then she grinned and wrote.

## Notes will does wonderous deliverings for friendlings!

Then she settled down on my pencil case (which was balanced on my lap to avoid icky toilet germs) and she watched me write.

(She really is the best.)

**Chloe,**

I've got so much news!!!

There's a new girl called Amelie and she's just like Emily, but Emily can't stand her! If Emily would just talk to Amelie, I'm sure they'd be best friends.

Tomorrow we're going to see some Egyptian stuff at the museum. I'm hoping Amelie and Emily bond over their love of poo beetles or something.

Also, Notes *really* wants to know who drew her (which is sad because how will we ever know?!). Oh, and there's a weird metal thing stuck in the ground.

See! So much news!  How about you?

**Molly xx**

Notes folded my note into a little aeroplane and hopped on. Then, with a wave, she flew up over the cubicle door and was gone.

I didn't hang about in the loos while I waited for her. That would be weird. Instead I went out into the sunshine and found my friends.

I joined a crowd from my class standing at the edge of the field, staring into the distance.

They were looking towards the holes. Not that you could really see anything from so far away. It was frustrating that we weren't allowed on the field.

That didn't stop us talking about it, though.

It's not fair.

What are they trying to hide?

I bet Mr Grimmers buried it.

I bet it's uranium.

What's uranium?

You don't know what uranium is?!

You don't either.

At least I've heard of it.

What if it's a sarcastigus?

What's that?

You mean a sarcophagus ... Like from Egypt? ... Nah, not in Bogdale.

*It's probably an old bit of pipe.*

(That was Amelie.)

Well, that's not very exciting.

*Just being realistic.*

(Amelie again.)

If it is an old bit of pipe, it's our old bit of pipe.

Yeah!

That was pretty much the conversation for the rest of lunchtime. I kept watching the sky, even though I knew it was unlikely Notes would get back so soon.

But just as the bell was ringing something papery landed on my head. Notes *was* back! And she looked exhausted.

Before even looking at Chloe's letter, I snuggled Notes into my pencil case with Captain Purrkins and a little heap of sharpenings.

Then I let the rest of my class walk ahead while I read.

# Whaaaat!?

MY CLASS IS GOING
TO THE MUSEUM
TOMORROW AS WELL!!!

I can't believe it! How crazy is that!?

Maybe I'll see you there!
Maybe I'll even help you talk some
sense into Emily!!
OK, so my news: they're called
dung beetles! Haha, trust you!

P.S. Let me know about the metal thing!

P.P.S. Poor Notes! I wish she had a little
paper witch family. I kind of feel like
she's the only one, though.

P.P.P.S. See you tomorrow! (Hopefully.)

Chloe was going to the museum?! Chloe was going to the museum?!! Best. News. Ever.

The afternoon whizzed after that. My mind was a total spinny whirlwind. And at the top of the whirlwind was one huuuuuge thought:

*I might see Chloe.*

# CHAPTER SIX

I didn't see Chloe.

At least not at first.

We had to sit on a very cold floor in a dark room, listening to a museum lady called Miss Terry.

She had all this white hair that stuck out like a cartoon character getting an electric shock. And she had this strange glass thing that's like glasses, but just for one eye.

Also, Miss Terry knew lots of gross (but also fascinating) facts. She told us loads about the ancient Egyptians and some other *very* interesting stuff too.

Here's my 'THINGS MISS TERRY TOLD US' top ten:

**10.** Egyptians invented the whole

# one year = 365 days thing.

(Which is totally weird. So before that did no one have birthdays?
Did no one know how old they were?!)

**9.** Ancient Egyptians also invented toothpaste!

PYRAMINT
TOOTHPASTE

**8.** (This is not an Egyptian thing but still to do with history.)

Miss Terry is old. She says she remembers the museum opening when she was our age and she's been working here for twenty-two years.

**7.** Most ancient Egyptian people didn't live past thirty-four years old.

(Miss Terry laughed when she told us that, but I'd have been worried if I was her.)

**6.** Ancient Egyptians used to put mouldy bread on icky infected body bits.

**5.** The 'glasses for one eye' thing is called a monocle.

**4.** Ancient Egyptians believed they could live for ever. When people died, they were wrapped up and made into mummies. Then their souls could hop back into their bodies if they wanted to.

**3.** Ancient Egyptians loved wearing wigs!

**2.** (This one is just crazy.)

Miss Terry knows Mr Stilton. OK, that bit's not that weird. But get this: she used to be his teacher at Dungfields!!! I DIDN'T EVEN KNOW MR STILTON WENT TO DUNGFIELDS!!!

Which brings me to ...

**1.** **But stop!** I can't just tell you number one. It's too amazing for that. I've got to explain it ...

So, we were already mind-blown about Mr Stilton going to Dungfields. And to be honest I guess it was a bit mind-blowing that he'd once been a kid.

young Mr Stilton

impossible to imagine Mr Cheesy without a beard

93

"Your teacher was a wonderful student. Such a kind, sensitive boy!" Miss Terry had said, and Mr Stilton shrugged and stared at his hands.

"Loved history, he did! Got so excited when we made that time capsule."

And we said, **"Huh?!"**

Then she said, "Oh, I'm sure Mr Stilton remembers. Buried it by that pretty little tree, we did."

And we said, **"The conker tree?!?"**

Then she said, "Well, yes, now you mention it,

I think it *was* a horse chestnut."

And Marvin called out,

# "WOW! KAPOW!"

And then everyone was talking so fast over the top of each other that no one could really hear anything at all.

"Silence, you horri— lovely children!" shouted Mr Stilton (or something along those lines because he was acting really odd).

Everyone stopped talking.

Then he coughed and gave Miss Terry one of those "read my mind" looks, and he said, "Shall we get back to ancient Egypt?"

But Miss Terry wasn't the mind-reading type, because she said, "Ah, yes, the time capsule. I remember it well."

And Mr Stilton flared his nostrils and gritted his teeth and said, "Well, *I* don't."

"Oh, you must!" said Miss Terry. "You were adorable that day when we were planning what to put in it! I remember you accidentally called me—"

"Nope!" said Mr Stilton. "I was *not* adorable, and this has *nothing* to do with ancient Egypt!"

I couldn't believe it. Teachers aren't supposed

to get snappy at other adults!

Miss Terry had *only* called him adorable. It's not like she'd called him a grumpfesting beard troll (which would have been much more accurate).

Notes' little mouth hung open in shock as she scribbled across the floor ...

What Mr Teachings is doing ?!

I didn't have a clue! All I knew was the metal thing in the field at school was a time capsule, and Mr Stilton really, *really* didn't want to talk about it. Which was a shame because I really, *really* did.

None of us kids made a single sound. We stared from Mr Stilton to Miss Terry and back again.

Miss Terry raised an eyebrow up high above her monocle and waited for Mr Stilton to say sorry. Which he did:

worryingly high — eyebrow ↑

"Sorry."

He mumbled it, staring down at his feet. And the scary thing is, he reminded me of me! I actually felt a bit bad for him. He just looked so awkward and embarrassed.

Miss Terry's eyebrow seemed happy with the apology. Anyway, then she let us hold some pretend ancient Egyptian jewellery, which was pretty cool.

And Marvin and Grace got to try on outfits.

Mr and Mrs Pharaoh

not typical ancient Egyptian fashion

After that, Miss Terry said, "All right, class! The museum is closed to the public today, so you're free to explore. Take a clipboard and paper. One between two. And

# don't touch anything!"

Which was an odd thing to say because everything was either behind glass or roped off. Plus, who'd want to touch that spooky stuff anyway? Not me.

As everyone got up, Mr Stilton looked weird (not unusual) and he was all quiet and non-bossy (VERY unusual).

Now, I am *not* Mr Stilton's biggest fan. And

neither is Notes (she calls him Mr Grumpings, Mr Grouchings ... stuff like that). But we both wanted him to be OK.

Notes wrote across the floor.

Mr Grumpings is also big mysterings! Maybees wants chats and listens and maybees yummy sharpenings?!

"Yep," I whispered. "I don't know what's wrong with him. But I don't think he'd tell me. We should probably just leave him alone."

(I ignored the thing about sharpenings.)

Notes wrote another superfast scribblenote.

Friendling Molly is probables right. Notes will keeps sharpenings. After all, Notes is needing tasty energies for puzzling Notes' big problem: WHO DRAWED NOTES?

Uh-oh. That again. She would never, *ever* know who drew her. I needed to just say it. But her little face was so hopeful. I didn't have the heart.

so very hopeful

Anyway, then someone tapped me on the shoulder, and I was (mostly) happy but (slightly) nervous to see it was Emily!

"Partners?" she said, not smiling but not frowning either.

(And, by the way, what was with all the crazy-confusing emotions???)

"Yeah," I said.

"I'll write," she said, already holding a clipboard and pencil. "You read out the questions from the class list."

Oh, this was going to be fun and not at all uncomfortable. ← sarcasm

I unfolded my copy of the class questions.
But to be honest I was more interested in finding
Chloe and/or getting to the bottom of Emily's
oddness. So I only pretended to look at the
questions. What was really happening was this:
Notes was looking at the questions while *I* was
looking for my bestie.

"We need to be in the next hall," I said.

"Why? What does it say?" said Emily.

"Come on!" I said.

"Read the question!" said Emily.

I didn't. Only one question mattered:

# WHERE WAS CHLOE?

And even though Emily was getting irritated, she followed me.

And it's a good thing too. Because **WHOOOOOP!** there in the next hall, by a big, colourful pharaohy thing, was a small group of kids. And right in the middle was ...

Chloe!

# CHAPTER SEVEN

"Isn't that Chloe?" said Emily. "Over there. Look."

"Oh yeah!" I said (like it was totally new news).

And I began walking over, but Emily grabbed hold of my arm.

"You can't just go over there!" she said.

"Why?" I said.

"She's with her class!" she said.

"So?"

"So, it's weird!"

I didn't really care about weird. I cared about seeing Chloe.

"Look," sighed Emily, "why don't we just stay close by, then when their group splits up, we'll go over?"

"Mmm-hmm," I said, but I had an even better

idea. I'd write a note to Chloe saying "Hi, I'm here", and get Notes to sneak it over to her.

But ... where was Notes?! I scanned the room. There were jewels and gold coins, chipped plates  and cracked bowls, mummies and coffins, cow-gods and cat-gods and bird-gods but no Notes!

I couldn't see her anywhere! Which was slightly worrying. Though maybe she'd also spotted Chloe. Maybe she'd gone to say "Hi". Yep, that was probably it.

So I did like Emily suggested and waited. Kind of.

Actually, I dragged Emily over to a big lump of stone, right near Chloe's class. And we sat behind it like spies.

*"This is ridiculous!"* whispered Emily.

*"It's fine! It's fine!"* I whispered back. *"We're just getting a close look at the high ... high ... picture things."*

"Hieroglyphics!!" hissed Emily. "Don't you know anything?! Can we at least look at the questions?"

By which point I'd had enough.

"Here's a question," I said (quite loudly). "Why is my normally nice friend Emily being so very *not* nice?!"

Emily gasped. "That's ... that's ... I don't know what you mean!" she said.

And I said, "Mean? Let's talk about *mean*. Ever since Amelie got here you've been the meanest meanie in Meanville!"

"What? I'm not mean!"

"You are, Emily. You're mean! Proper mean!"

I had totally shocked her into silence. I felt

powerful. Like I was Ra the Sun God, thwacking

people with sunbeams.

Molly Ra →

But here's the thing – it was too much Ra. *Far*

too much Ra. And now I was the mean one.

## Argh.

And Emily still wasn't saying a single word.

"Molly?"

It was Chloe. And – oh, perfect – half her class. "Molly? What are you doing down there?" she said.

I looked at Chloe and I looked at Emily.

Emily's bottom lip was wobbling.

"Just give me a min with my friends?" Chloe said to her classmates, and they shrugged and headed off to look at the exhibits.

"What's going on?" she said once they had left.

I hugged her like we were long lost twins, separated at birth, finally reunited. And then I stopped because I needed to say something important.

"I shouldn't have said that," I said to Emily.

"No, you shouldn't have," she said.

So I said,

I'm really sorry.

And I thought she'd ignore me or go off in a huff, but she didn't do either of those things. She started crying.

"It's true! Everything you said. It's all true!"

Emily blubbed. "I've been vindictive and malicious and—"

"I didn't say those words," I said.
(I don't think I even *knew* those words.)

Chloe coughed. "Emily?" she said. "What's up?"

And then – at last – finally, finally, *finally* ... Emily explained.

"OK," she said. "So, when this new girl, Amelie, arrived, I recognised her from a chess tournament last summer. She'd beaten me and at the time I was fine with that. I just thought, *Here I am, good at so many things. Who cares about chess?*"

Emily sniffed and dabbed her eyes on her sleeve.

"And then when she said about her judo brown belt, well, then I started to worry a bit. Because, Molly, I don't know if you've noticed, but Amelie is a bit like me. She's like me but better. More confident, more interesting, more facts on ancient Egypt, more friends! Even *you* prefer her to me. Be honest."

I stared at her. "I honestly think ... you're an idiot."

"See!" wailed Emily, and Chloe gave me a "why did you say that" glare.

"What I mean is, you're an idiot if you think someone's better than you just because they know more, or just because they've done more. That's just – just – idiotish!" (Possibly not a real word.)

She sniffed again and looked at me through watery eyes, like she still wasn't sure if I was being unkind or not.

"Emily," I said, "I like you – we all like you – for being *you*. Not because you're the best at stuff. You know this, right?"

She nodded. "I do. Most of the time. I suppose I was just jealous. I'm so embarrassed."

I nodded. "I've not experienced that myself," I said, "but it sounds horrible."

Chloe gave me another look. It was a look that said "you have to be kidding me".

(I may have accidentally turned into a horrific jealous terror when Chloe left.)

"Fine," I said. "Emily, don't worry about it. We all get jealous sometimes. Even me. *Especially* me."

"Really?" she said.

I nodded.

"I think
I need to say
sorry," said Emily.

She hugged Chloe and said, "Thank you,"
then left to look for Amelie.

*Huh!?* I thought. *What about my "thank
you"?*

And Chloe started giggling because she could
see from my face that I was a bit miffed.
(Miffed is what my nan calls me when I'm a tiny bit annoyed.)

miffed →

"You're unbelievable!" laughed Chloe. "You're jealous because Emily thanked *me* for helping *her* get over being jealous!"

Hmm, well, when she put it like that ...

"Haha, OK, fine!" I said. "I'm over it. So, do you want to look around together? I kind of want to see what Notes makes of it all."

"Definitely," said Chloe. "Feels like ages since I saw her. Where is she?"

It took me a moment to understand. Did she mean Notes? But Notes was with her, wasn't she?

"She's not with you?" I asked, already
knowing the answer.

We'd both stopped smiling now. And as Chloe
shook her head a horrible panic settled in my
tummy like an ice cube sinking into a glass of
squash. Because if Notes wasn't with me and she
wasn't with Chloe, then where was she?

# CHAPTER EIGHT

I should probably explain. It's not that Notes can't be trusted on her own. She totally can (ish). Like when she flies between our schools she's always alone (except for Captain Purrkins, of course) and that's fine. But the museum was different. (And when I say "different", what I really mean is so extremely creepy!)

Everything seemed to be about death.

jar for keeping gross body parts in

stone from a tomb (where they kept dead people)

cat mummy (actual dead cat inside)

bird mummy (actual dead bird inside)

Sarcophagus
(best not to think about what's inside)

So I really didn't like the thought of Notes being lost around all this creepy stuff. Because even though she's a witch, she's not exactly a spooky one.

## Oh, where was she?!

A knot of worry twisted in my tummy. She was so fixed on solving the mystery of who had drawn her. Had she flown off to find an answer?

But it was an impossible puzzle! I hated to

think of her confused and disappointed, crying papery tears into Captain Purrkin's slightly weird rubbery fur.

Chloe squeezed her eyes tight shut, the way she does when she's trying to remember her times tables. "OK," she said, "I'm a little paper witch with magical powers ..."

"You feeling OK?" I said.

Then she said, "Shhhh. It's what detectives do. I'm getting into Notes' head. Working out what she's thinking."

"Oh. Well, can you do it quickly?" I said.

"Because we need to start looking."

Chloe ignored that.

"I is Notes," she said in a voice that was both squeaky and freaky. "What is I likes doing most in whole wondrous world?"

Well, that was ... bizarre. I was pretty much too weirded out to speak. (Unlike Chloe.)

"Some helpings, please, friendling Molly?" she said.

And I said, "Only if you stop doing that voice."

"Hmph. Fine."

So with Chloe being Chloe again, I thought about her question: what *did* Notes like doing best of all?!

"She likes eating pencil shavings," I said. "And she loves writing – obviously – and flying, of course ... And she always wants to be helpful. Oh, and just lately, when she's bored, she's started doing this thing where she hangs dustballs off Mr Stilton's beard. It's very artistic."

"That's it!" she said.

"Really? The beard thing? You think!?"

She shook her head. "No, not the beard thing, the helping thing! Notes is wondrous helpingful."

I gave her a "please not again" stare.

"Sorry," she mumbled. "But the point is, Notes likes helping. So she's probably doing something to try to help you *right now*. What do you need help with?!"

I couldn't think.

"What do I need help with? Nothing. Everything. I don't know! I suppose there's this?"

I showed Chloe the question sheet. "Maybe she's flown off to do my work for me!?"

Yikes. It's always a worry when Notes decides to help. Though I liked this idea *slightly* more than the thought of Notes searching. I couldn't stand to think of her sad, little face as she tried (and failed) to find whoever drew her. The schoolwork theory was definitely better.

Chloe looked at the question sheet. "Makes sense," she said. "She's probably somewhere nearby, answering all these questions. Phew. I know it's silly, but I was starting to panic a bit."

"Me too," I said.

Chloe was right, though. It was just like Notes to fly off and do my work for me. I was stressing over nothing.

"Ha!" I laughed. "What are we like, eh? So dramatic and ... and ... What's that, though ..."

Notes had scribbled something on the bottom of the paper.

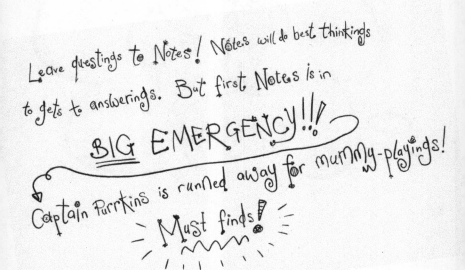

Leave questings to Notes! Notes will do best thinkings to gets to answerings. But first Notes is in BIG EMERGENCY!!! Captain Purrkins is runned away for mummy-playings! Must finds!

"Mummy playings???!" I hissed. What did *that* mean??

"You ... you don't think Captain Purrkins is playing *with* a mummy, do you?" said Chloe.

"Nah," I said. "He wouldn't. That's just so—"

"Disgusting, yeah, I know," said Chloe. "But this is Captain Purrkins we're talking about. Captain Purrkins who plays with dead flies for fun."

This was true. Captain Purrkins is both cute and gross.

Chloe gulped. "I don't want to see Captain Purrkins playing with a mummy."

I didn't either!

"You know ... Maybe I should go and find

Emily. Make sure she's OK," I said.

"And I should probably join the rest of my class," said Chloe.

But we couldn't just abandon Notes, could we?!

"No," I sighed. "Notes is our friend. We have to help her. She'd help us."

I stood, proud like a soldier, my eyes all full of strength and determination and honour and other soldiery stuff. And that's when a paper aeroplane landed on my foot.

It was a map of the museum!

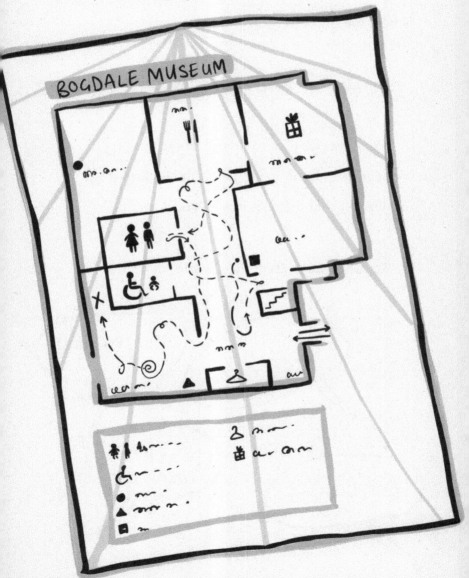

"It's from Notes," I said. "She's showing us where she is!"

"Do you think she's trapped??" said Chloe.

There was no time to lose! If Notes was trapped, we had to get to her!! The problem was, we weren't that great at map reading.

So, while we walked, there was a lot of this:

Also, kids from
my class kept
getting all excited
when they saw Chloe.
It was like she was famous.
Kids who never even used to talk to her were
getting all squeaky and bouncy. So our map
reading kept getting interrupted.

Also, we had to avoid Mr Stilton and Chloe's teacher because we were both meant to be writing stuff down about ancient Egypt.

Anyway, eventually we decided we were in the right spot. Or, should I say, the right *pot*? (Haha.) Because that's where we were. Next to a massive pot.

(Notes had actually scribbled an X on the floor, so that was a bit of a clue!)

An old photo
next to the pot
showed a woman
digging the
pot out of the
ground. It made
me think of our

time capsule
treasure back at
school, waiting to be dug up.

Anyway. "Psst! Notes!
You there?" I said.

We stared at
the pot. Nothing
happened.

"Maybe we're too late," said Chloe. "They probably left ages ago."

But then something happened. A little papery witch zoomed out of the pot. And at first I was all "yay" and "phew", but then I was all "uh-oh" because ...

"Something's wrong with Notes!" said Chloe.

The witch hovered in front of us, holding a note, and Chloe was right. Everything about her was wrong.

Notes was an ancient Egyptian! And that's not all. Something had happened to Captain Purrkins. Something totally horrible.

He pulled himself up on to the rim of the pot then leapt on to the reedy thing.

Beside me I heard Chloe's breath, all shaky and sad.

Captain Purrkins was a mummy!!!

# CHAPTER NINE

OK, that's not quite true.

We *thought* Captain Purrkins was a mummy.
He wasn't.

Here's what happened.

Chloe was this close to crying. And I was
jibber-jabbering.

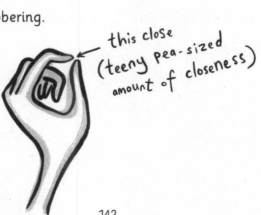

this close
(teeny pea-sized
amount of closeness)

"OK. Right. *OK.* Captain Purrkins is a mummy. A mummy. OK. Right. Oh dear. I don't like this, Chloe. I really don't like this, Chloe. I don't like this at all, Chloe. He's a mummy, Chloe. Captain Purrkins. A mummy, Chloe. A mummy!!!"

(I may have been very slightly panicky.)

And then a scrap of crumpled paper came flying out of the pot.

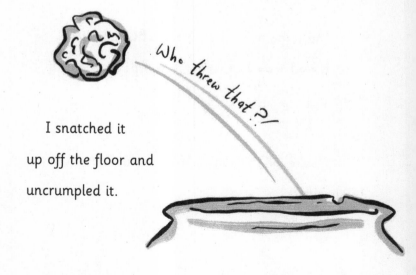

Who threw that?!

I snatched it up off the floor and uncrumpled it.

"Notes!" gasped Chloe.

And a moment later, Notes (ACTUAL Notes, not the witch we *thought* was Notes) popped out of the pot.

"You're OK?" I said. "And ... and Captain Purrkins?"

Captain Purrkins jumped up out of the pot with a happy "mew".

"But if you're you, then who ... who are they??!"

Notes hopped down and scribbled on the museum floor.

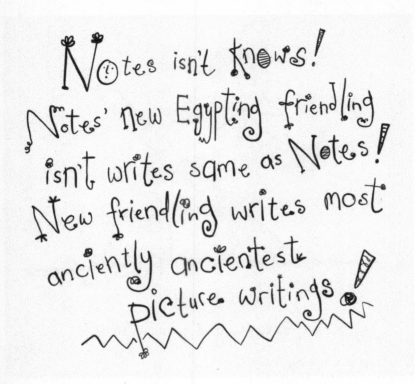

Notes isn't knows! Notes' new Egypting friendling isn't writes same as Notes! New friendling writes most anciently ancientest picture writings!

"Hieroglyphics," said Chloe. "That's what it's called."

The ancient Egyptian witch smiled and nodded.

"You can understand what we're saying?" I asked.

She nodded again.

"And Notes' notes? You understand those too?"

Her smile drooped as she shook her head.

"But if Notes can't write in hieroglyphics, and you can't write in English ... How can you talk to each other?"

She scribbled something on the floor in hieroglyphics. (Which didn't help much.)

Luckily Notes was also scribbling ...

Notes and new friendling
can does wondrous mimings
and goodly doodlings! Is how I
telled new friendling that Chloe
and Molly is also Notes' friendlings!
Is how new friendling knows
you is kind and
trusty secret-ers!

Notes fetched
a doodle, one
she'd done earlier.
It showed me and
Chloe (I think).

So she'd drawn us smiling to show her new friend that we could be trusted. Which is all great, but what about this new friend? She *seemed* friendly but what did we really know about her?!

I wrote a private note to Notes.

How do you know she's kind and ~~trustly~~ ~~trustworthy~~ trustworthy?! Look at her cat! It's cute but also a bit gross, don't you think?!

The little mummy cat was now balancing on the rim of the vase, bopping Captain Purrkins' tail. And, OK, perhaps it didn't *look* all that

gross, but it was still A MUMMY!!!

Notes laughed and started writing a reply. But I couldn't read it straight away because Chloe elbowed me. "Over there, look!" she said. "Emily's coming back."

Yep. A very gloomy-looking Emily was shlomping towards us.

"Oh, hi," I said, trying to sound all extra normally normal. (It's really hard acting normal when you're thinking about ancient Egyptian scribble witches and their creepy mummy pets.) "What's up?"

Emily sniffed. "Amelie is avoiding me! I found

her in the gift shop. I went over to her to say
sorry but the moment she saw me she left."

"Ooh, gift shop!" I said.

"Molly!" said Chloe.

"Oops," I said. "I mean, I'm sorry about
Amelie. Do they have any pencil toppers?"

"Molly!!!" said Chloe.

"Fine. Sorry. I bet they do, though," I said,
and Chloe shook her head at me (even though I bet
she was just as excited as I was).

Anyway, then Emily said, "Well, actually ..."
And she pulled a brand-new pencil topper and
notepad out of a paper bag.

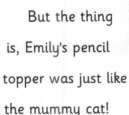

"I was so miserable
about Amelie," she said.
"I couldn't resist."

But the thing
is, Emily's pencil
topper was just like
the mummy cat!

"Phew!" said Chloe.

"Oh. Ah ... Haha ... I get it!" I said.

(I couldn't help it!)

"What?" said Emily.

## Oops.

"Nothing," I said. "Just ... good."

She gave me a funny look, but I was too relieved to care. The cat mummy wasn't a cat mummy. It was a cat mummy pencil topper. Which was not at all gross and actually very cool.

On the floor, Notes hopped up and down, pointing at her writing.

Cat mummy is pencil toppings like Captain Purrkins!

Apparently our little mummy mistake was hilarious.

"What? What are you two smiling at?" said Emily.

"Oh ... nothing, nothing ..." I said.

Meanwhile the mini cats were rolling about, play-pouncing on each other. And Notes' new friend was teaching Notes an ancient Egyptian dance.

"Seriously, you two! You're grinning at nothing." Emily frowned. "It's like the old days, back in class. You two and your secrets. Me not knowing what's so funny all the time."

Which made me feel **SUPER GUILTY.**

"Sorry," said Chloe *(who obviously felt super guilty too).*

Time to change the subject.

"Amelie," I said.

"What?! Where?" said Emily.

"No, I mean—" What did I mean?!

"You ... you should write to her!" said Chloe.

"Yes!" I said. "Exactly. Explain why you've

been a bit ... you know ..." (I didn't say the word "mean" again, but she knew what I meant.)

This was a brilliant idea for two reasons.

**1.** Emily actually did need to explain to Amelie.

**2.** We kind of needed some alone time with Notes and her friend.

Chloe must have been thinking the same thing. "Why don't you use that new pencil and pad. You could sit in that comfy-looking seat over there. Take your time. Write a really long sorry letter."

Emily was still frowning but in a thoughtful way, not a grumpy way.

"That's actually a good idea," said Emily. "I won't be long!"

"Don't rush it!" said Chloe as Emily hurried off, all determined.

Chloe looked at me and I knew exactly what she was thinking because I was thinking it too. We were being all **us against Emily**, and it wasn't a great feeling. But we didn't have much choice.

Notes has to stay secret. It's really important. She's only small and she's super fragile so we can't take any risks.

Anyway, Emily could really do with a best friend. And Amelie was the perfect fit. Like Cinderella's shiny slippers. 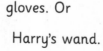 Or Elsa's anti-magic gloves. Or Harry's wand.

Or Superman's bright red pants.
Or maybe not the pants, but
you get my point.

We were doing Emily a favour.

Kind of.

Ish.

# CHAPTER TEN

So, OK, I felt a bit bad about sending Emily
away, but we had a situation happening.

Up until now, we'd thought Notes was the
only scribble witch. One of a kind. Unique. The
one and only. But here was another scribble
witch, right in front of us. All ancient and
mysterious.

I sooo wanted to know more about her,
but she was impossible to understand. What
we needed was someone who could read
hieroglyphics. But who knew that kind of thing?

Except Emily probably *did* know that kind of thing, and we'd just sent her away!!

Would it be so wrong to interrupt her writing? Maybe I'd just go over and ask her to jot down a quick ancient Egyptian alphabet?!

Nope, the letter was important to her.

If only I could think of someone else like Emily.

"I've got it!" I said.

And Chloe said, "Great! What have you got?"

"Amelie!" I said.

"You've got Amelie?!" said Chloe.

"Yes! I mean – well – no. But Amelie's going
to help us."

Notes scribbled on the ancient pot.

Truthfuls?!
New Emily will fix all Mysterings?
New Emily will mend Mr Grumpling's sads?
New Emily will finds answer to
where did Notes come from ?!

Oh dear. She was getting her hopes up again.

"Sorry, Notes. I don't think Amelie can do those things."

Her teeny shoulders slumped.

"But she might be able to tell us what these symbols mean. Then we can work out what your friend is saying," I said. "Worth a try?"

Notes thought for a moment then unslumped herself.

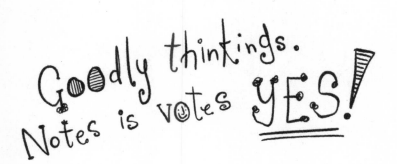

Goodly thinkings.
Notes is votes YES!

Her friend hopped off her reed pen and
scribbled on the ground. (Without any ink!)

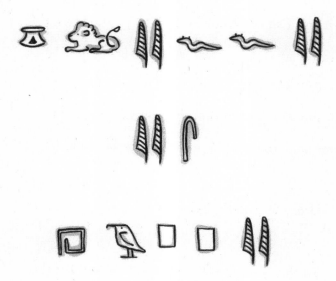

(Which we couldn't understand but
at least she was trying to join in.)

"OK, let's go find Amelie!" I said.

But then Chloe said, "I think I should find my class."

And I said, "What? Why?!"

And she said, "I won't be long. I just need to show up, see my teacher, let her think I'm working. You should probably do the same."

Urgh. She had a point.

So this is what we did. I went to find Amelie (and figured I'd say a quick hi-bye to Mr Stilton too). Chloe went off to find her teacher. The witches and cats stayed at the big pot. And we agreed we'd all meet back there as soon as possible.

Amelie was in the next room, and she was really easy to find because she'd started giving guided tours. (I'm not even joking.)

A little group of Dungfields kids was trailing around behind her, taking notes, looking really impressed. I joined them.

"Ah, see here," she said, pointing into a cabinet of gold jewellery. "These are on loan from the British Museum! Now *that's* a museum. And look – look at the markings on the rings. Interesting. I don't recognise the hieroglyphics."

"So you do recognise *some* hieroglyphics?" I said.

They noticed me then.

"It's Molly! **KAPOW!**" grinned Marvin.

I grinned back.

"Oh, hi, Molly," said Amelie. "Yes, obviously I know some glyphs."

I knew it!

"And, of course, we've got these," she said, and she waved a bit of floppy card at me.

"Huh?" I said.

"Look!"
said Marvin,
whooshing an
identical piece of
card through
the air.

"Flying ancient Egyptian higher-glifics!

NEEEEEEEYYYYOOOOOOOW!"

"We've all got them," explained Alfie. "We can *all* read hieroglyphics!"

Suddenly everyone seemed to be waving floppy cards.

"Huh?!" I said again.

"Only free thing in the gift shop!" said Mia.

(Something free in the gift shop??
I so needed to go to the gift shop!)

"What is it, though?" I said.

"Bookmark," said everyone.

And that's when Mustafa let me look at his. And all I'll say is this: I had to have one!!!

How insanely perfect was that!? It was just what I needed.

"Amazing!" I said. "I'm getting one!!!"

There were lots of cringey awkward faces when I said that. Faces that looked like they were about to give me really bad news. It was unsettling. Something bad was coming.

Like ...

**"Sorry, Molly. Your favourite gerbil fell down the plughole!"**

Luckily I don't have gerbils.

Or ...

*"Sorry, Molly. All your pencil toppers have been stolen by an evil stationery-burglar."*

Or ...

*"Sorry, Molly. You've got a spelling test."*

(Urgh – I shouldn't even joke about that last one.)

"You can't," said Amelie. "I'm sorry, Molly. They're all gone."

WORST. NEWS. EVER.

"NOOooooooooooooooooooOOOOOooooooo oooOOOOOOoooooOOOOOOOOOOO OOOOOOOOoooooOOoooooooooOO oooooooOOOOOOOOOOOooooooooo!"

I groaned, falling to my knees with my head in my hands. (Thinking about it, this was possibly a slight overreaction.)

Hush fell like an avalanche. (A really quiet museum-based avalanche.)

173

I heard someone murmur, "I guess she really likes hieroglyphics."

Then I heard Mr Stilton's big clompy shoes.

"Molly, get up. What are you doing?"

"Nothing," I said, clambering up.

"And what *should* you be doing?" he said.

"Erm," I said.

"The class questions, Molly? You *do* remember the questions, Molly?" (It's always a bad sign when he says your name too many times.)

And then he said, "I will be expecting to hear your answers to our class questions later, Molly. Understand, Molly?"

And I said, "Oh, definitely." Even though I hadn't answered any questions on account of all the **much more important** things I had to do. (Gah! To think I felt sorry for him!)

Anyway, he plodded off and I started begging my friends. "Please!" I said. "Someone! Anyone! Pleeeease let me borrow one of those bookmark thingies!"

But the thing about kids is the more other kids want stuff, the more valuable stuff becomes. (I know this because I am a kid, obviously.) So then everyone was clutching their bookmarks to their chests like they were tickets to an all-you-can-eat chocolate chompathon.

"OK," I sighed, turning away.

*I'll just have to go back to Notes empty-handed,* I thought.

But just when I'd given up, Amelie did something heroic (again). "Here," she said. "Take mine."

"Really?!" I said, hugging her. "I'll bring it straight back!"

She shook me off. Possibly Amelie isn't the huggy type. "It's fine, you can keep it. I know the symbols anyway."

Then she leaned in close and whispered so the others couldn't hear. "You do know it's just a bit of card, don't you?"

I grinned and nodded. I felt puppyish. All light and bouncy and happy. If I had a tail, I would have wagged it.

But there wasn't time for imaginary tail-wagging.

I had places to be and ancient Egyptian

mysteries to solve!!!

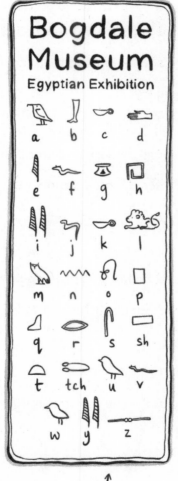

# CHAPTER ELEVEN

"I've got it!" I said to the big pot. "Look!"

Four little heads popped up.

I held out the bookmark so they could see.

Notes clapped. The Egyptian witch did an ancient Egyptian happy dance.

Then they both climbed down and started scribbling on the floor.

**Such wondrous findings!!**

(I read Notes' note aloud so her witchy
friend could understand.)

"OK ... wait a minute ..."

I pulled out my little notebook and my favourite pen from my dog pencil case.

Then I concentrated.

If ▨ meant "**Y**"

and ▨ meant "**E**"

and ⌠ meant "**S**", then ... **YES!**

She was saying "yes"!

I wondered when Chloe would get here. She had to see this!

Emily was still across the room, writing her letter to Amelie (how long did that letter need to be?!), but Chloe was nowhere. I kind of wanted to wait for her but didn't want to waste time. So I decided to start asking the Egyptian witch some questions!

"What's your name?"

(That seemed like an important one.)

" **G-L-I-F-F-Y** ... Gliffy?" I said.

"Like hierogliffy? Cool name."

Notes hopped up and down and pointed at the floor. She had questions of her own, and – again – I read them ...

Is you anciently and wiseful?

"**O-L-D** ... Old! I guess that's a yes."

Is you has wondrous magics?

Gliffy pointed to the mummy cat pencil topper and nodded.

"Of course," I said. "She's like you, Notes. You both do magic with stationery!"

But then Gliffy wrote this.

"**T-E-L** ... **H-I-D-N** ...
**S-E-C-R-E-T-S** ... Tell who? I don't
understand."

And then she did something that made my
mind go **KABOOM**. She closed
her eyes and started writing. And this is what
she wrote:

"**B-E-S-T** ... **F-R-E-N-D** ...
**P-E-N-S-L** ... Huh?!"

OK, so the kaboom didn't happen straight away. But a second later Chloe hurried into the hall holding a paper bag.

"Sorry I'm late. Was at the gift shop!" she said.

"What? You went to the gift shop without me?!"     (Slightly annoying but not really the point.)

"Yeah," she said. "Sorry. My whole class was in there so ... But look!" She pulled out a shiny pencil and waved it at me. "Cool, huh?"

**KABOOM**

not very Egyptiany but still cool ↝

"You knew!"

I said to Gliffy.

"How did you ...?!"

Gliffy tapped her **T-E-L** ... **H-I-D-N** ... **S-E-C-R-E-T-S**

note again like she was trying to

explain.

"*Tell hidden secrets?* So you can just

magically know stuff that's hidden to everyone

else?"

She nodded.

"Like a fortune teller?!"

"**I-SH**... Ish? Ha! You mean kind of?"

Another nod.

# THiS WAS MASSiVE!!!

I had to sit down otherwise I swear I'd have fallen over.

Then, while I explained everything to Chloe, Gliffy and Notes started writing to each other (I let them see the bookmark so they could translate).

"Whoa!" said Chloe. "She knew I had this?! What else does she know?"

Hmm. Good question.

"We should ask Gliffy something really extra important like ... like ... why can't I think of anything?"

Notes tapped Chloe on the shoulder then wrote on the floor.

Notes did ask Gliffy **big** questings! Here is Notes' top ten findings: ← (Haha! Good to see Notes was getting into the top ten thing too!!)

10. Gliffy friendling is drawed on specialist papyrus paperings.

9. Gliffy is travels with ancient Egyptings exhibition and is goes to museum then other museum then more museum and ons and ons...

7. Gliffy is teller of secret mysterings!

5. Gliffy is promises magic posty-card sends to new best friendling (Notes)!

4. Gliffy is knows who is Gliffy's mummy! Gliffy's mummy dids drawed Gliffy two thousand years ago. And Gliffy's mummy is now bandagy Egypting mummy!

1. Gliffy is can writes super-speedish like Notes. (Is how we did wondrous fastly writings!!!)

I made a mental note to help my scribble witch friend practise her counting.

Then I whispered something to Chloe. This was the whisper:

*"Do you think Gliffy could tell us who drew Notes?"*

I didn't want Notes to hear and get her hopes up. But how cool would it be if Gliffy *could* help?

*"I don't know,"* Chloe whispered back. *"I guess we could try?"*

But before we had a chance to ask, Emily appeared. "It's no good!" she said.

Emily held out a handful of scrunched-up notepaper pages.

"What do you mean?"

I took one of the papers and read ...

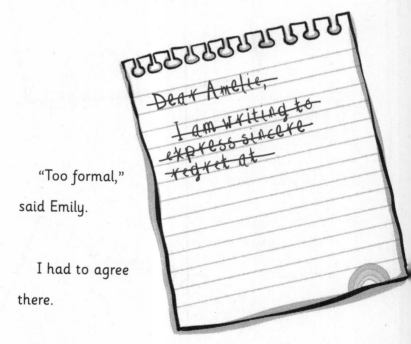

Dear Amelie,
I am writing to express sincere regret at

"Too formal," said Emily.

I had to agree there.

I took another.

doesn't
sound
anything
like her!  →

Hi!

~~Big soz for being~~
~~such a loser!~~

"Too casual!" said Emily.

She wasn't wrong.

The next was also very

un-Emily-ish ...

~~Hey, girl!~~
~~My bad!~~

"Too cheerleader," she said.

And the next reminded me of a certain teacher.

"Too Stilton," Emily said with a cringe.

There were more notes (*lots* more) but we didn't have all day. And anyway, the problem was really, *really* clear!

"Emily," I said. "You just need to be yourself."

Amelie,
~~I've been~~
~~such a~~
~~horrible~~
~~snottling!~~

She sighed and shook her head. "I know. It's just not that easy."

"Erm, Molly ..." Chloe tapped me on the shoulder. "We may have a problem."

She held out another note.

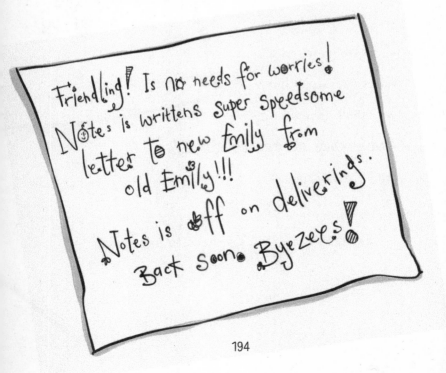

Friendling! Is no needs for worries!
Notes is writtens super speedsome
letter to new Emily from
old Emily!!!

Notes is off on deliverings.
Back soon. Byezees!

"I couldn't stop her," said Chloe. "She gave me the note and then she was gone! It was all so quick!"

"Don't worry," I said. "It's not your fault."

When Notes wants to do *helpings* there's not much anyone can do to stop her.

# CHAPTER TWELVE

"Er ... Molly? Chloe? Can we focus on my problem a moment please?" said Emily. "I don't mean to be all me, me, me, but it's quite urgent!"

I looked at Chloe. Chloe looked at me. And I just knew she was thinking the same thing as me. This was Emily's problem. And it was more urgent than ever!

There was only one thing for it. We had to find Amelie and we had to find her fast!

"Let's go!" said Chloe.

"What about Emily?" I said. Should we leave her here? Take her with us?!

"Let's just go and get this sorted, agreed?!" said Chloe. She looked all determined, like an explorer from the **Mysteries of Ancient Egypt** book. The one who dug up King Tutan-thingie's tomb.

Anyway, we linked arms with Emily and kind of marched her out into the next room, where Amelie was standing.

Standing ... and also reading ... and also looking more than a little bit confused. Unknown to Amelie, Notes was sitting on her head, looking pleased with herself.

When Amelie saw us she held out Notes' note.

Dear new Emily,
I is sooo sorrying for my badly means! Please can we be best friendlings for ever and ever? friendling hugs! from your newest best friendling, old Emily

"Who's new Emily?" she said. "I don't get it. Is this supposed to be funny?"

Yikes! I snatched the note and scrunched it into my fist, needing it to go away!

Emily opened her mouth like she was going to say something, but no words came out. I guess she was too horrified to talk.

Notes tilted her head to one side and lifted her shoulders in a confused shrug. I'd just have to explain to her later.

"Yes!" I said. "I wrote it! I was being funny. I'm always being funny, aren't I? That's me! Funny old Molly!" I tried to laugh but it sounded a bit scary, so I stopped.

Aha...
aha ha...
hm.

Emily looked a mix of confused and critical. Like maybe I was trying to trick her (which I was but in a good way).

"Anywaaaay ..." I said, "old Emily — I mean, *just* Emily — wants to say something. Isn't that right, Emily?"

Emily shot me a dangerous glare. Then she sighed.

"I ... Yes. I want to say something."

Chloe and I stared at her, nudging her with our eyes

(but not really because that would be gross).

"I'm sorry," said Emily. "I'm
sorry for being unfriendly.
I ... I was jealous of you,
I think. Because you're
cleverer than me. And
because everyone thinks
you're brilliant. Which you
probably actually are. So ... that's all really.
I'm sorry."

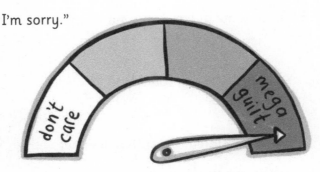

don't care

mega guilt

# SORRY-O-METER

There was an awkward silence before Amelie
finally spoke.

"OK," she said.

Then she walked away.

And if the silence *before* she left was awkward, then this *new* silence was awkward with extra awk.

"It'll be OK," I said to Emily.

"I thought you were my friend," she said.

And for a moment I didn't get it. "What do you mean?" I said. But, of course, it was obvious. "Oh, that ... that wasn't me! I mean, I know I said it was, but it really wasn't ... I can't explain but you have to believe me."

Emily sighed. She looked really tired. Then she went away, saying she needed to write up some notes.

# Urgh.

Mr Stilton marched around the museum soon after that, giving us a five-minute warning.

# Double urgh!

That left us hardly any time to say goodbye to Gliffy (and only a crazy-quick trip to the gift shop for me afterwards).

This is my super-speedy gift shop top five (because there wasn't enough time for a top ten):

## 5. Bogdale Museum pencil sharpener

← boring but handy

## 4. Hologram scarab ruler

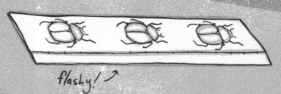

flashy! ↗

## 3. Tutankhamun pencil case

so... much... gold...

## 2. Pharaoh pencil topper

I bought one →

## 1. Cat mummy pencil topper

has to be number one for obvious reasons ↗

Anyhow, getting back to the goodbyes ...
Chloe and I took Notes back to the big pot (we explained about the Emily situation on the way) and Gliffy flew over to join us.

"Sorry, Gliffy, but I've got to go soon. Chloe

can stay a bit longer, I think. And Notes can too if she wants."

Captain Purrkins and the mummy cat were playing so happily that it seemed wrong to separate them so soon.

Notes wrote on the floor:

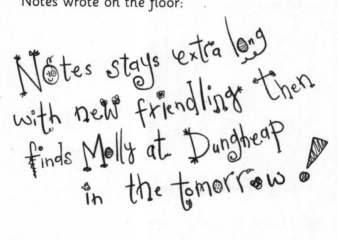

Notes stays extra long with new friendling then finds Molly at Dungheap in the tomorrow!

Well, I guess that was fair enough.

"It's been amazing meeting you. I hope you and Notes can keep in touch," I said to Gliffy.

"**W-I-L** ... Will. You will?" I said, and she smiled and wrote this:

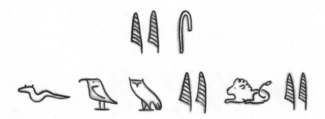

"**I-S F-A-M-I-L-Y** ... Is family? You mean Notes is family? That's so ... so ..."

(But I had to stop talking or else I'd have blubbed.)

I said a sad goodbye to Chloe and tried not to let any tears drip on the paper witches.

The other kids from my class were gathering around Mr Stilton and Miss Terry by the exit, and I joined them. I stood with Emily (who was very quiet) and Marvin (who was less quiet).

Mr Stilton counted our heads to make sure no one had got stuck in the loos or been eaten by mummies. Then we said "thank you" to Miss Terry before trudging back to school.

What you looking at?

Annoyingly, there was just enough school time left to discuss our class questions. And extra annoyingly, Mr Stilton wanted me to join in.

"So, Molly," he said, "what kind of ancient Egyptian objects have been found by archaeologists?"

Argh! I just didn't know ... Or did I?

"Pots?" I said. "And papyrus ... And reed pens for writing in hieroglyphics."

"Good," he said. But I wasn't finished.

"Although sometimes they carved into stone instead."

"Thank you, Molly. Anyone else want to comment?"

"And cat mummies!" I said. "They loved cats."

Mr Stilton held up a hand to stop me. "Thank you," he said again, and this time I stopped.

Anyway, my point is, I got away with not trying to learn stuff because I accidentally learnt stuff (and accidental learning is way better).

Emily and Amelie sat next to each other at our table (they didn't really have a choice) and it was soooo uncomfortable because neither of them spoke to the other. And I was relieved when home time came and I could finally escape.

On the way out, Amelie caught her huge bag on the door handle and all her stuff went flying out.

Emily helped pick up all the bits, but she didn't say a single word. And Amelie only said *one* single word. ("Thanks".)

So I guessed it was just one of those things. Amelie and Emily were never going to be friends.

# CHAPTER THIRTEEN

Sometimes I love being wrong. Actually, that's not true. But this time I did.

So, this is what happened the next day, and it still makes me smile just thinking about it.

It was break time and the sun was shining and, best of all, we were allowed on the field. Which, for my class, meant one very important thing: it was time to dig up the time capsule.

Notes was back but she wasn't herself. She was very quiet. Which is an odd thing to say because she's always quiet. But she wasn't even writing many notes.

All she wrote was this:

Gliffy telled Notes most BIGGLIEST EVER tellings!!!

And then nothing.

It was like she was in shock, but she wouldn't explain it.

Anyway, break time arrived, and my class was

all **"YEAH, WHOOOOP! TIME CAPSULE TIME!"**

Though we didn't say anything about this to Mr Stilton.

Everyone (including Emily) headed out to the spot by the tree where the hole was. (The rain had caked the time capsule in mud again but at least we still knew where to look.) Emily watched from the back of the crowd.

Mia had found a big stick and she gave it to Amelie because Amelie was our official archaeologist. And that's when the happy thing happened.

"Emily should do it," Amelie said, "if she wants to?" And she said it all calm and cool, but it wasn't calm and cool. It was

# sunshiney wonderfulness.

It was Amelie's way of saying, "We *can* be friends." Like she wasn't really offering a stick at all. She was offering a tiny little (imaginary) friendship-seed and asking if Emily wanted to plant it.

And it was such a huge relief when Emily smiled and took hold of the stick. Because it was like the friendship-seed had been planted!

(Well, that's how it seemed to me anyway.)

No one else really got the Emily/Amelie drama, but *I* got it and so did Notes. I could tell Notes understood, because even though she was all weirdly quiet, she still gave my nose a happy hug.

Then Emily started digging. It was harder this time because the ground was all dried up and she had to really jab the stick in hard. But then there was a **CLACK** and we knew she'd hit the time capsule. So after that she dug even faster because we were all so excited to see what was in it.

I lik skool so mush!

And finally Emily stuck her hand in and pulled and pulled and out it came!

She shook off the dirt and (after a LOT of straining) unscrewed one end.

Here's what was inside: pictures, notes, diary pages! All from different children.

Today our class had the computer all day!

by Je

This BE

Dear children of the future.
Today (a long tim...

**My best day**

Today is my best day.
This is because I laughed so
much. I laughed until I
thought I'd throw up
(but I didn't! Ha!)
I laughed because Jon
~~axidently~~ accidentally
called Miss Terry MUMMY!
He was so embarrassed!
Hahahahaha!!!! by Tony

Doodly style a
LOT like Notes!?

Me
by Jon.S

...me
...I fell off.

...s in
...s.
...idea.

by Sadie

Who is Jon?! →

My news by Nikita
Today I walked to
school with Becky
we had chewy
sweets and Becky
said they tasted like
dog biscuits and I
liked them so maybe
I should try dog
biscuits
the end

familiar
scribbles ↑

Custard
our class
tortoise

YUM

...Day by Dorek
...was so funny
...Miss Terry
...MUMMY and the...

Me at the seaside
by Raj

Notes was very still as she looked at Jon's doodly face. She just kept staring and staring at it.

"You OK?" I whispered but she didn't answer.

Anyway, Emily said we should probably take all this stuff to show Mr Stilton because it was kind of partly his. And Amelie said that was a smart idea.

(yas!!! Hello teeny sapling friendship!)

Mr Stilton had definitely been a bit weird about the time capsule back at the museum. And some of us (me) thought we should absolutely one hundred per cent NOT show him in case he went all Mr Cheesy-Grumptastic again.

Then Emily and Amelie tutted, and they shared a look. It was a funny little eye-rolling look that seemed to say, "There she goes again. Typical utterly ridiculous Molly."

(Rude, huh? But I was so happy to see them getting along that I actually didn't mind. That's how good a person I am.)

Anyway, after break we all carried bits from the time capsule back to class.

We spread everything out on Mia's table because that's closest to the front of class. And when Mr Stilton saw he went very quiet. Even though there were loads of questions flying at him like cannonballs.

WHEN?

WHO?

HOW?

He ignored them all. But then Emily asked, "Which one did you do?" And something changed.

It was like he'd been bothered by something and he'd only just realised how silly it was.

Because he smiled. **Mr Stilton!** He actually smiled. And then he said, "That's me, there. Jon." (And he pointed at a doodly drawing ... the one that looked oddly like Notes!)

Then Mia said, "So you're the one who—"

"Accidentally called his teacher 'Mummy'? Yep. That's me."

Everybody kind of half laughed. It *was* funny, but we weren't sure if it was allowed to be funny. And then something happened ...

**HA HA HA!**

"I called Mrs Banton 'Dad' once," said
Mustafa.

"I called Mrs Oddments 'Gran'," said Harry.

"I called you 'Mum' once," I said to Mr Stilton.
"But no one heard!" Which was true. I'd got
away with it at the time, but I suddenly felt like
confessing too!

**HA HA HA!**            **HA HA!**

And then Mr Stilton started laughing. "I can't
believe how embarrassed I was," he admitted,
and we all joined in laughing too. Because if you
can laugh about something, then it *stops* being
embarrassing. Which is brilliant if you think
about it.

**HA HA HAHA!**

**HAHA HAHA!**            224

**HA HA HA!**

Anyway, while all this was happening,
something was going on with Notes.

No one had noticed (including me) but she'd
been writing on the whiteboard with an actual
whiteboard pen!

Mummy will bees OK!

It wasn't long before kids saw.

"Huh?! Did you write that, Mr Stilton?" said
Grace.

And when Mr Stilton saw it, he pretty much

went back to his normal grumpy self, because Mr Stilton NEVER lets anyone write on the board without asking.

"Of course I didn't. **Senseless nonsense!** Back to your seats, foul snottlings!" he said.

To be honest it was good to have him back to normal, though. Nice Stilton was unsettling.

It was a funny thing for Notes to write but at least she was writing again. That was a big relief!

For some reason she spent a long time hugging Mr Stilton's nose after that, while we went back to our tables. Which was odd.

I'm 99% sure he didn't notice ↓

Notes has never been Mr Stilton's biggest fan (I'm not even sure he has any fans) so what was she up to?!

She's very strange that scribble witch. But that's part of what I love about her.

Oh, also, I found this in her pen pot. I guessed it had to be the note from Gliffy. The one that made her act all funny.

I couldn't find my bookmark, though, so I didn't know what it said!

Back at our table, Marvin was busy bobbing to a song he'd got stuck in his head, while Emily and Amelie were cracking Tutankhamun jokes no one else understood.

definitely getting bigger

Now, I'm not nosy (just to be clear) but I may have listened in to a bit of their conversation while I pretended to tidy my pencil case:

"I remembered you from the chess thing too," said Amelie.

"You did?" said Emily.

"Of course," said Amelie.

Silence. *Uh-oh*, I thought. (I wondered if their friendship plant was wilting already ... Can imaginary things wilt?!)

Then eventually Emily said, "Well, that's embarrassing."

But Amelie said, "Why?! You did so well. And I remember you saying you only practised at weekends. I have to practise every day to be this good. And it's stopped being fun! I hate it!! I'm always so worried about losing."

"Oh," said Emily. (More silence.) Then she said, "I think ... maybe ..."

"What?" said Amelie.

At this point I stopped pretending not to listen.

"What??" I said.

Emily sighed. "I think maybe I worry a LOT about losing too. With everything. Not just chess. And then lots of stuff stops being fun."

I nodded. "Yeah. You should TOTALLY be more like me. I *never* worry about losing. It's great."

They both looked at me. It was *that* look again. The "utterly ridiculous Molly" look.

Then they lowered their voices to a whisper so I couldn't listen in.

# Charming!

But at least the Emily-Amelie friendship plant was doing OK. *More* than OK. And that's what mattered. (Though I will stop being so kind and understanding if they get too "utterly annoying".)

I really was happy for them, though. Emily deserved a best friend, and she'd finally found one!

And while they were busy being besties, Notes was busy being bonkers.

She was whizzing in circles around Mr Stilton's desk, and I swear she was letting him see her, every now and then. Because Mr Stilton was getting proper jumpy.

Notes was zooming down right into Mr Stilton's eyeline. And each time she did he flinched.

Then, one time, Notes hovered in the air, right in front of old Cheesy's face! And his face did this ⟶

What was she thinking!?

Eventually she flew back over. She looked exhausted.

"What's going on?!" I whispered.

She just smiled, and she pointed to the note from Gliffy.

"I don't know what it says!" I whispered. But I don't think she heard me. She had already curled up with Captain Purrkins next to my pencil case. And she was snoring.

I was going to have to wait to find out about Gliffy's note. So I decided to write a little note of my own.

Chloe,

We can write again! yay!!! And here's my ultra-extremely exciting news ... We dug up a time capsule! It was full of letters and drawings and there was even one by Mr Stilton when he was a kid.

Everything's a bit odd but also kind of great. Emily and Amelie are friends!! And Notes is being all funny with Mr Stilton. I'm not really sure what that's about!

Anyway, everyone is OK, the sun's shining and wondrous happy!!!

Loads of love and hugs!

Molly xx

# THE END
(Kind of.)

P.S. Dear Reader,

It's me, Molly. I still can't find my bookmark. But if you've got one, then maybe you could work out what Gliffy said to Notes?! Every time I ask Notes about it, she just giggles! (Silently, though. You know what she's like!)

Anyhow, thanks for reading!

Big hugs!!

From
Molly Mills xx

P.P.S. This just landed on my desk out of nowhere!!

no address!?

P.P.P.S. I found my bookmark!!!!! This is what Gliffy's note said (I've written it upside down and backwards so you'll have to stand on your head and use a mirror ...)

You're WELCOME. Love, Mr Stiffon !?

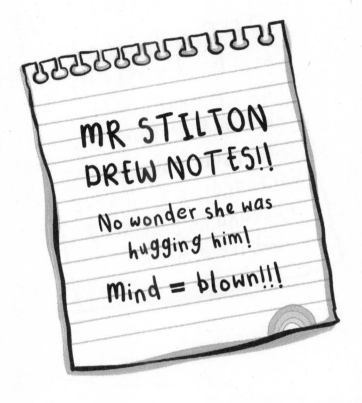

p.p.p.p.s. (This really is the end now.)

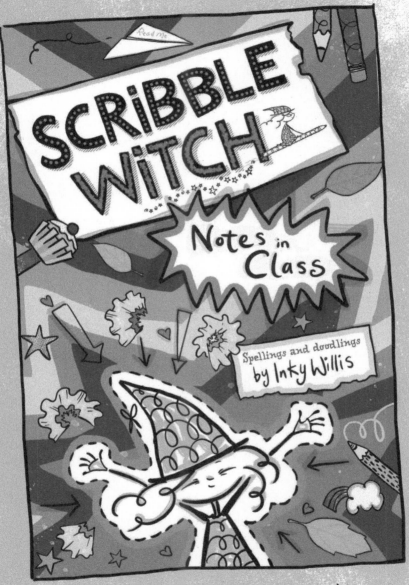

Have you read all of the
SCRIBBLE WITCH books?

# SCRIBBLE WITCH

## Magical Muddles

Spellings and doodlings
by Inky Willis

Cut out your own bookmark and try writing a secret message using only hieroglyphics!

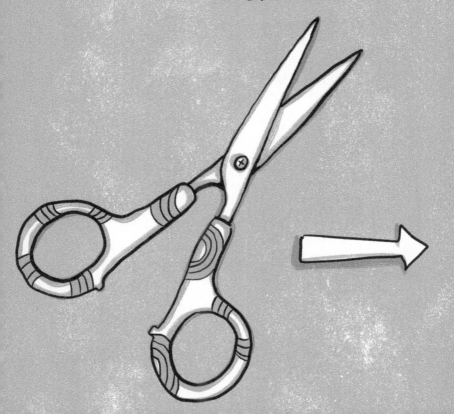

# Bogdale
# Museum
### Egyptian Exhibition

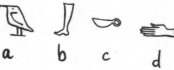

a    b    c    d

e    f    g    h

i    j    k    l

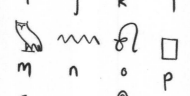

m    n    o    p

q    r    s    sh

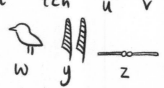

t    tch    u    v

w    y    z

# How to draw:
# SCRIBBLE WITCH

★ Start with these basic shapes

1.
2.
3.
4.
5.
6.
7.
8.

← Ta-da!